W9-AUX-165

BEAUTIFUL MOON
BELLA LUNA

Written by/Escrito por
Dawn Jeffers

Illustrated by/Ilustrado por
Bonnie Leick

County of Los Angeles Public Library
Canyon Country Library
18601 Soledad Canyon RD.
Canyon Country, CA 91351
(661)251-2720
JUN 02 2010

Text © 2009 Dawn Jeffers
Illustration © 2009 Bonnie Leick
Translation © 2009 Raven Tree Press

All rights reserved. For information about permission to reproduce selections from this book,
write to: Permissions, Raven Tree Press, a Division of Delta Systems Co., Inc., 1400 Miller Parkway,
McHenry, IL 60050 www.raventreepress.com

Jeffers, Dawn.

Beautiful Moon / written by Dawn Jeffers; illustrated by Bonnie Leick, translated by
Eida de la Vega = Bella luna / escrito por Dawn Jeffers; ilustrado por Bonnie Leick,
traducción al español de Eida de la Vega. – 1 ed. – McHenry, IL ; Raven Tree Press, 2009.

p.:cm.

Bilingual Edition   English Edition
ISBN 978-1-932748-87-1 hardcover   ISBN 978-1-934960-05-9 hardcover
ISBN 978-1-932748-86-4 paperback   ISBN 978-1-934960-06-6 paperback

SUMMARY: What if days went on forever and nighttime never came?
         Find out what a girl does to fill her days and fulfill her dreams.

Audience: pre–K to 3rd grade.
Bilingual full text English and Spanish and English–only formats.

1. Bedtime and Dreams--Juvenile fiction. 2. Bilingual books. 3. Picture books for children.
4. Spanish language materials—Bilingual. I. Illus. Leick, Bonnie. II. Title. III. Title: Bella Luna.

Library of Congress Control Number: 2008932223

Printed in Taiwan
10 9 8 7 6 5 4 3 2 1
First Edition

Free activities for this book are available at www.raventreepress.com.

Raven Tree Press
A Division of Delta Systems Co., Inc.
www.raventreepress.com

To my little rays of sunshine
Ryan, Isabella and Sophia.
With love, Aunt Dawn

Para mis pequeños rayos de sol,
Ryan, Isabella y Sophia.
Con amor, Tía Dawn

To my parents, for giving me moonlit
woods and sun drenched fields.
Love, Bonnie

Para mis padres, por darme bosques iluminados
por la luna y campos inundados de sol.
Con amor, Bonnie

The sun sets.
The grass is cool.
I look into the dark indigo night and
see the glow of the beautiful moon.

El sol se pone.
La hierba está fresca.
Miro la noche de un índigo oscuro
y veo el resplandor de la bella luna.

But I am restless in the darkness.
There is still so much to do.
I need a day that never ends.

❧

Pero estoy inquieta en la oscuridad.
Todavía hay mucho que hacer.
Necesito un día que nunca termine.

The moon flashes a smile.
In a wink, the sky begins to peel away.

❧

La luna me dirige una sonrisa.
De pronto, una esquina del cielo se levanta.

I take an edge of the nighttime sky.
I pull until the sky is full of light.
The sun wraps its warmth around me.

Agarro un borde del cielo nocturno.
Tiro de él hasta que el cielo se llena de luz.
El sol me envuelve con su calor.

I run
and swim
and eat
and play.

Corro
y nado
y como
y juego.

12

13

Birds chirp.
Animals roam.
Flowers stretch in the sunlight.

❧

Los pájaros trinan.
Los animales corretean.
Las flores se desperezan bajo la luz del sol.

I play until I am too tired to go on.
I sit to rest and look around me.
Something is very wrong.

Juego hasta que ya no puedo más.
Me siento a descansar y miro a mi alrededor.
Algo no está bien.

The trees hang low from too much sun.
The grass turns brown in the constant heat.
I am tired, but can get no rest.

❧

Los árboles se encorvan por tanto sol.
La hierba se torna marrón bajo el calor constante.
Estoy cansada, pero no puedo descansar.

I always wanted a day that never ended,
but now I know better.
Nighttime is the time for rest,
a time to gain energy for a new day.

❧

Siempre quise que el día no terminara nunca,
pero ahora comprendo algo.
La noche es para descansar,
el momento de obtener energía para un nuevo día.

The sun smiles.
In a wink, the bright sky turns
back into a blanket of indigo.

❧

El sol sonríe.
De pronto, el cielo brillante se
convierte en una manta índigo.

The moon smiles.
And in a wink —

La luna sonríe.
Y de pronto —

The stars sparkle.
The animals rest.
The trees and flowers cool.

Las estrellas centellean.
Los animales descansan.
Los árboles y las flores se refrescan.

The sun sets.
The grass is cool.
I look into the dark indigo night and
see the glow of the beautiful moon.

❧

El sol se pone.
La hierba está fresca.
Miro la noche de un índigo oscuro y
veo el resplandor de la bella luna.

Life is as it should be,
just me and my beautiful moon.

❧

La vida es como debe ser,
sólo yo y mi bella luna.

Vocabulary | Vocabulario

Vocabulary	Vocabulario
beautiful	bella
moon	la luna
darkness	la oscuridad
day	el día
sky	el cielo
birds	los pájaros
animals	los animales
flowers	las flores
sunlight	la luz del sol
trees	los árboles
grass	la hierba
stars	las estrellas